Splish, Splash

By Christine Economos
Illustrated by Pat Paris

ISBN 1-58120-049-8

1 2 3 4 5 6 7 8 9 CL 03 02 01 00

"Look, Sara," said Carlos. "Pop's Movie House is holding a talent show. It's just for high school kids. Just think. We could both be in it. With our talent, we might win. What do you say?"

"A talent show? Sure, we could be in it," said Sara. "There are just two things that would not work. One, we don't have much talent. People would laugh at us. And two, I can't think of one thing we could do."

"No one is going to laugh at us," said Carlos. "We both have a lot of talent. We can do a song. We can do <u>Splish, Splash</u>."

"Say we did have talent and a song," said Sara. "We would also need a name."

"I know a good name. How about Laugh and a Half? That would be a good name," said Carlos.

"Laugh and a Half? No way!" said Sara. "Let me think. How about Half and Half? That is a much better name. I'll let you be the first half. What do you think?"

"Fine," said Carlos. "One more thing. If we win, we each get a movie pass. It's good for a year. We can see as many movies as we want."

"A movie pass is a good thing to have. I just hope our friends don't laugh at us," said Sara.

"What is that song?" asked Dad.

"It's <u>Splish, Splash</u>," said Dan. "Carlos and Sara are doing that song for the talent show. It's at Pop's Movie House. A lot of their high school friends will be in the show, too."

"Carlos and Sara both have talent, but they might not win," said Dad. "Their high school friends have a lot of talent, too. Carlos and Sara need to work a lot more if they want to win."

"They have put a lot of work into that song. They have some time left. They'll do just fine," said Mom. "We should all go to the show. It would be a lot of fun. Then we can all clap for Carlos and Sara. We can bring them good luck."

"We both did a lot of work on the song," said Sara. "But we need to make it better. We can't just stand there like two lumps."

"We did rush into this," said Carlos. "I wish we had a lot more time to work on it."

"We don't move when we do the song," said
Sara. "We need to move. How about clapping
our hands? What if we tap our feet like this?
We can move our feet from side to side like
this. Does that look better?"

"We can do that. That makes the song much
better," said Carlos. "We'll clap our hands.
We'll tap our feet. We'll move from side to side.
We'll be a hit! We'll bring down the house!"

"Did you see Sara's good-luck shoes, Nina?" asked Dan. "She will not go to the talent show without them. She has looked all over for them. So have I. Sara is in a big rush. She can't be late."

"Sara's shoes were a mess," said Nina. "They looked like they had junk on them. I gave them a bath. I hope they aren't too wet."

"Will you tell Sara or should I?" asked Dan.

"What did you do to my shoes, Nina?" yelled Sara. "This one is dripping all over!"

"I wanted you to look your best," said Nina.

"I need these shoes for good luck," said Sara. "I'll just have to do the song with wet shoes."

"Sara! You're late! Where have you been?"
asked Carlos. "I thought I would have to go
on without you. Look at your shoes! They're
dripping wet. Don't drip on me."

"I will not drip on you," said Sara. "I could not
find my good-luck shoes. Nina had them. She
thought they were a mess. So she used water
on them. Then I had to rush over here with
wet shoes. But I could not go on without my
good-luck shoes. What did I miss?"

"Not much," said Carlos. "Some kids did songs. Others did jokes. The songs were good. But people didn't laugh at the jokes. We'll do our best, but we might not win."

"I hope I can tap with wet shoes," said Sara.

"Here comes Half and Half," said Dan. "Come on. We should clap."

"I hope they do well," said Dad. "But look at Sara. She's splishing and splashing all over the place."

"Sara's shoes splish and splash each time she taps her feet," said Mom. "Water is dripping off the shoes as she moves from side to side. But it looks like she's doing it for the song."

"The people are laughing," said Nina. "They like the song. They like Carlos and Sara."

"If people laugh, they might win," said Dan. "We should clap. If we're clapping, other people will clap, too. Then they'll win for sure."

"We came in first," said Carlos. "Now we'll each get a pass to Pop's Movie House."

"You'll take me, right?" asked Nina. "I was the one who gave Sara's shoes a bath. I put the splish splash into your song!"

New Skills and Vocabulary

vowel:
long i spelled igh

consonants:
spl, th

additional skill:
double final consonants before adding verb endings

decodable words:
both, clapping, dripping, high, might, splash, splish

sight words:
house, move, water

story words:
half, shoe, talent

ISBN 1-58120-049-8

90000>

9 781581 200492

FIDGET SPINNER

50 AWESOME TRICKS

INCLUDES COOL FIDGET SPINNER